ENID BLYTON LIBRARY

Titles in this series

The Rude Little Rabbit
The Lucky Green Pea
The Pixies and the Primroses
The Tale of Scissors the Gnome

ISBN 0-86163-639-2

Text copyright 1945, 1949 Darrell Waters Limited
Illustrations copyright © 1994 Award Publications Limited

Enid Blyton's signature is a trademark of Darrell Waters Limited

First published 1949 as A Story Party at Green Hedges
by Hodder and Stoughton Limited
This edition first published 1994

Published by Award Publications Limited,
Goodyear House, 52-56 Osnaburgh Street, London NW1 3NS

Printed in Belgium

# Enid Blyton

# The Rude Little Rabbit

*Illustrated by Rene Cloke*

AWARD PUBLICATIONS LIMITED

There was once a little speckled rabbit called Bobtail who was very rude. He called cheeky names out after anyone he met and he always answered back when anyone scolded him.

"Hello, pins and needles!" he would say to Prickles the hedgehog. Prickles always got very much annoyed when anyone called him that.

"I shall tell your mother," Prickles said.

"Tell my father and my mother, my
brothers and my sisters, my
grandmothers and my grandfathers, my
great grandmothers and my great
grandfathers!" Bobtail said.

"I suppose you
think you're
clever," said
Prickles.

"I don't think it,
I know it!" sang
out Bobtail.

Then he saw the beautiful kingfisher fly
down from the tree. The blue and green
bird was dazzling to look at, but he hadn't
much of a tail, which always made him feel
a bit sad.

"Left your tail at home this morning?"
asked Bobtail popping his head out of a
bush.

"If you were my child I'd spank you and put you to bed," said the kingfisher annoyed.

"If I were your child I'd find you a new tail and stitch it on!" said Bobtail rudely.

But one day he was
rude to the wrong person!
He was rude to the
Spotted Goblin who lived
in the hollow oak tree.

The spotted Goblin had once dropped a pot of red paint and it had splashed up and spotted him with red all over. As it was magic paint, he hadn't been able to wash it off, so had to leave the spots for always.

Bobtail saw him coming along and he pulled his whiskers and thought of a joke. He knew that measles had spots so he called out after the goblin:

"Hello, Measles! How are your spots?" The Goblin turned round and glared.

"If you dare to say that again I'll put a spell on your ears!" he said.

Bobtail didn't believe him. "Hello, Measles, how are your spots?" he said again, and then rushed off to his hole at once.

"Kikky, rooni, billiboona!" shouted the Goblin in an angry voice. It was a spell for rabbits' ears but Bobtail didn't know it.

The spell worked. When Bobtail got to his hole
and tried to flatten his ears down over his head as all
rabbits must do when they run underground, Bobtail
found that he couldn't put his ears down at all! No, they
stayed upright. It was strange.

He tried to force his way into the hole. His mother saw him, and spoke to him sharply. "You've left your ears up. Put them down, silly child."

"I can't," said Bobtail, in dismay.

"Don't be stupid!" said his mother. "All rabbits can put their ears down."

But Bobtail couldn't. It wasn't a bit of good. His ears stayed straight up, and even when his mother tried to bend them down she couldn't. She only made Bobtail cry out with pain.

"Well, you can't come into the burrow unless you put your ears down," said his mother. "You'll wear them out. What have you been doing to get your ears like this?"

"I was rude to the Spotted Goblin," said Bobtail, looking ashamed. "I said: 'Hello, Measles, how are your spots?'"

"What! You were as rude as that!" cried his mother. "I'm ashamed of you. You deserve to have a spell put into your ears, you really do."

Well, poor Bobtail had a bad time after that.
You see, he couldn't dash into his hole with all the other
rabbits when an enemy came along. Sometimes it was a
sly fox, coming to get a young rabbit for dinner.
Sometimes it was a dog hunting. Other times it was a
farmer with a gun.

Bobtail dashed into the bushes, but it was easy for foxes or dogs to smell him out. He ran and ran and they ran after him. He only managed to escape by leaping into a hollow tree and staying there quite still whilst his enemies rushed past.

"This is dreadful," thought poor Bobtail. "What a life I shall lead with ears like this. I never knew before how important it is for a rabbit's ears to be able to flop over."

One day he saw the Spotted Goblin standing at the top of Steep Hill, Bobtail made his way humbly to him.

"Please, Spotted Goblin," he said, "I'm very sorry I was rude to you. Take the spell out of my ears. I'll never be rude to anyone again."

"I can't take the spell out," said the Goblin. "There's only one way of curing those long ears of yours – and that is to throw you from the top of the hill to the bottom!"

"Oh no, oh no!" cried Bobtail, wishing he had never gone near the Goblin.

But the Spotted Goblin lunged out with his foot and gave Bobtail a hard kick.

He rolled down the hill,
over and over, over and
over, head and back
and heels and ears and
back and tail, over and
over.

His ears were bent and he squealed in pain. He lost two whiskers. He hurt his foot. He bruised his bobtail – and he certainly bent his ears back until they nearly broke!

He sat up feeling very shaky, at the bottom of the hill. He felt himself all over to see if he was still there.

Two young rabbits came out to
look at him.

"Do you usually come down the
hill like that?" they said.

"Now don't you be cheeky!"
said Bobtail, and he turned to
chase them. They went down their
hole – and he followed them.
Half way down he stopped
in delight.

"My ears are
all right again! They
bent themselves down
when I went into the hole.
Oh good – now they are cured!"
    But it was a very painful cure,
for Bobtail was so stiff and bruised for days
after that he could hardly lollop in and out of his hole.

"I hope you are cured of your rudeness now," his mother said to him.

"Mother, I'm the very politest rabbit that ever was," said Bobtail.

"What a change!" said his mother. And it certainly was!